ABOUT THIS BOOK

The characters for this book (girl, baby, hamster, and awful Benny Hogarth) were drawn by hand with pen and ink and gouache on Arches hot-pressed watercolor paper. The backgrounds, monkeys, and various boring adults are a digital collage of sampled watercolor washes done in Adobe Photoshop using a Cintiq 13 HD tablet.
The text was set in Sofia Pro Soft, and the display type is Nanami. The book was edited by Erin Stein and designed by Liz Casal. The production was supervised by Nicole Moulaison, and the production editor was Christine Ma.
This book was based on a book with the same title published by Idiots'Books in 2010.
If this isn't your book, please leave it right here. No excuses, no lies. No *ifs*, *and*s, or *maybe*s.
Please know we're not joking. The warning is clear—this book is protected by hamsters and babies.

Imprint
A part of Macmillan Children's Publishing Group

BABIES RUIN EVERYTHING. Text copyright © 2016 by Matthew Swanson. Illustrations copyright © 2016 by Robbi Behr.
All rights reserved. Printed in China by RR Donnelley Asia Printing Solutions Ltd., Dongguan City, Guangdong Province.
For information, address Imprint, 175 Fifth Avenue, New York, N.Y. 10010.

Our books may be purchased in bulk for promotional, educational, or business use. Please contact your
local bookseller or the Macmillan Corporate and Premium Sales Department at (800) 221-7945 ext. 5442
or by e-mail at MacmillanSpecialMarkets@macmillan.com.

Library of Congress Cataloging-in-Publication Data
Names: Swanson, Matthew, 1974– author. | Behr, Robbi, illustrator.
Title: Babies ruin everything / Matthew Swanson ; illustrations by Robbi Behr.
Description: First edition. | New York : Imprint, 2016. | Summary: "A big sister becomes
convinced her new baby brother is ruining everything"—Provided by publisher.
Identifiers: LCCN 2015022327| ISBN 9781250080578 (hardback) | 9781250085962 (e-book)
Subjects: | CYAC: Babies—Fiction. | Brothers and sisters—Fiction. | Humorous stories. | BISAC: JUVENILE FICTION / Family /
New Baby. | JUVENILE FICTION / Family / Siblings. | JUVENILE FICTION / Humorous Stories. |
JUVENILE FICTION / Social Issues / Emigration & Immigration.
Classification: LCC PZ7.S9719 Bab 2016 | DDC [E]—dc23
LC record available at http://lccn.loc.gov/2015022327

Book design by Liz Casal
Imprint logo designed by Amanda Spielman

First Edition—2016

1 3 5 7 9 10 8 6 4 2

mackids.com

BABIES RUIN EVERYTHING

BY Matthew Swanson   ILLUSTRATED BY ROBBI BEHR

[Imprint]
MAKE YOUR MARK
New York

My baby brother was born today. I know because Dad woke me up in the middle of the night.

He drove me to my grandma's house
and told me I would be a big sister soon.

I told him I didn't *want* to be a big sister.
Not even a little. But, apparently, I don't get a vote.

At Grandma's, the TV is too small,
the milk tastes weird, and it's
not okay to make yarn forts
in the living room.

While Mom and Dad and the baby
have a party at the hospital,
I am forced to play checkers
and eat cold oatmeal.

When Dad finally picks me up, he does not say hi to my hamster, Leonard. Instead, he tells me three hundred things I do not want to know, like how much the baby weighs, how big his head is, and how cute he looks when he wrinkles his nose.

Mom says I have to be nice to the baby, but it's very, very hard. He can't do a single useful thing.

He can't stand on one foot.

He can't catch a Frisbee.

And he can't *whistle*! Even big-head Benny Hogarth can whistle, and he already lost his front teeth!

Mom and Dad have a party
for the baby with balloons
and streamers and pointy hats.

The baby doesn't say thank you
for the party. He refuses to eat
his cake. He won't even open
his presents.

Clearly, there is something wrong with this baby.

I beg Mom to send him back, but
she shakes her head and says to me,
"He's just a baby, after all."

They put the baby in my room. Even though he's very small, he has a lot of stuff.

A picture of three kittens and a fuzzy pink walrus hangs where my "Types of Deadly Spiders" poster used to be.

I explain that my room is too small for me and Leonard and the baby—that maybe the baby should live in the kitchen.

But Mom and Dad do not agree.

The baby grows.

He learns how to sit,
but not very well.
He learns how to eat,
but he spills food all
over the place.
He learns how
to pick things up,
but then he throws
them at me.

Why am I the only one who sees the truth?

WE NEED A BETTER BABY!!

I want to go to the playground and
swing from my ankles, but Mom says,
"The baby is taking a nap."

I want to go to the zoo and see the
monkeys eat bananas, but Dad says,
"The baby needs his bath."

Instead, we watch boring shows where nothing ever happens.

Instead, we go to the baby store and buy ten gazillion diapers.

Instead, we have to whisper while playing Zombie Attack.

Leonard and I start a club for people who don't like babies, but Mom says I have to let the baby join.

NO BABIES

We start another club for people with moms who don't understand how clubs are supposed to work.

The baby loses the keys to the car, so no one can drive me to big-head Benny Hogarth's birthday party. I don't like Benny, of course, but I still want to go to his party.

There will be ponies at the party. And three kinds of ice cream. And a piñata shaped like a cowboy.

"Try to remember that he doesn't know any better," says Mom. "Try to remember that he's just a baby."

But he's NOT just a baby. He is a monster!
An abomination! A creature from the deep!
He wrecks my stuff. He cries all night.
He does not understand the importance of parties!
It's completely clear, without a doubt, that . . .

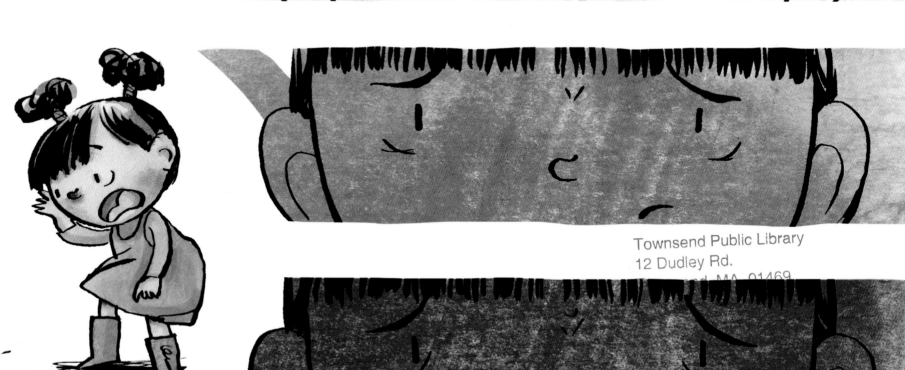

It suddenly occurs to me that maybe this baby just needs a better sister. So I decide to try something new. I try being nice to the baby.

But then Mom gets mad at me
for being nice.

Mom may not see it, but this baby has potential. He's related to me, after all. So I decide to teach him everything I know.

I teach him the planets and the months and the difference between frogs and toads, and my favorite letters of the alphabet. I tell him about spaceships and volcanoes and icicles and eggplants and all the kinds of trucks I can remember.

This baby is pretty darn smart. It's clear he knows that I'm the greatest sister in the world.

The baby and Leonard and I start a club
for people who like marshmallows.

The baby and I want to go to the zoo.
Mom and Dad say we can't, because it's raining.

The baby and I don't care about the rain. We want to see the monkeys eat bananas. We want to see them *now*.

There are two of us and two of them. Mom and Dad are no match for the baby and me.

We go to the zoo, and it's raining.

The monkeys refuse to eat their bananas. The baby cries and screams and ruins everything.

But I don't mind.

He's just a baby,
after all.